Prescott Red —
Dog Daycare Academy

Mary C. A. McNamara

To order additional copies of this book, contact:

1-888-795-4274
www.Xlibris.com
Orders@Xlibris.com

ISBN: Softcover   978-1-6698-3494-6
        EBook   978-1-6698-3495-3

Print information available on the last page

Rev. date: 08/11/2022

Dedicated to Meggy Gray and her golden
lab, Casey Jane - swim dog!

The little red dog with a black tail and a few fleas was not a city dog, he was a farm dog, but nevertheless, when harvest season came on the farm, Mr. and Mrs. Dachshund sent him away to stay with his Aunt Silver Dapple in the suburbs of a great big city.

It was a prestigious place of sorts, with patches of green throughout, shaded by large leafy trees, but mostly the new planned community where Aunt Silver lived was full of cement! Prescott did not mind — he thought walking on it would be good for his toenails.

Each morning, Aunt Silver would promptly leave at 7 o'clock for her important job in the city, and return late in the day just after 6 o'clock. "Well, hello, Prescott," she would always say on arrival, "How was your day?"

Prescott would just look at her and bark. *How does she think my day was?* Prescott would wonder in amazement.

It was a dismal existence for the little red dog with a black tail and a few fleas. He was use to roaming a farm all day, not stuck in a condo, and at Condo Plaza, the neighbors were not too friendly, nor did they appreciate seeing him out each evening for his walk even if he was on a leash! They thought he would ruin the community flower beds, which Prescott tried his best to stay clear of.

"It is time for dog daycare!" Aunt Silver finally announced one evening. "Inside a condo is simply no place for a little red dog with a black tail and a few fleas to spend the day."

The very next morning, Prescott found himself standing outside the gates of "Dog Daycare Academy." He suddenly wished he was back at Condo Plaza — even his fleas stayed home today!

Then out of nowhere, white tight curls, with long painted toenails in every shade of the rainbow came running over to great him. "Hi, I'm Polly! What is your name, handsome?" "Prescott Red," the little red dog shyly barked back in his best bark. "Well, welcome, Prescott, or should I call you Red? Do you want to play?" And with that, she bit him right on the rump and the chase was on!

DOG DAYCARE ACADEMY
A World Without Howls Is A World Without Happine

In a flash, four paws turned to eight, then twelve, then sixteen, for not only was the little dog with tight curls chasing him, but a speckled spaniel and an eager beagle as well!

In the yard, Polly soon introduced him to the other little dogs and the big dogs too.

The other dogs were excited to have a new dog at dog daycare and happily barked, "Welcome Prescott!"

Then Miss Pitt blew her whistle loud and all the dogs lined up
for the dog daycare song:
   "If you're happy and you know it bark out loud,
   If you're happy and you know it howl out loud,
   If you're happy and you know it, your tail will surely show it,
   If you're happy and you know it bark out loud . . .
   Woof, woof, woof, woof, woof, woof, woof!
   A woo, a woo, a woo, a woo, a woo, a woo, a wooooooooo!"

The bell then promptly rang and all the dogs scattered, but one little dog stayed behind to bark at Prescott. He then followed Prescott to his first class. Prescott did not mind, *he's a barker*, Prescott thought.

In his first class, Prescott learned the importance of barking in complete sentences, which he found the barker was good at!

Geography taught him there is more than one way around flower beds.

At recess, Polly met him for a nutritious snack and the barker joined them then barked at him all the way to arithmetic.

"You have 22 spots, Spot. Sims has 31, so, 31 − 22 = bark, bark, bark, howl: 9. Sims has 9 more than you, Spot!" The barker barked at Prescott in agreement.

At lunch, all the dogs were given their happy dog lunch boxes and woofed them down!

Then one wolfhound howled out the dog pool cry, and the race was on to the pool!

Prescott sprinted on over with the rest of the dogs, but when he reached the gate, the swim instructor, Miss Casey Jane gruffly barked, "Where is your swim certificate little dog?" Prescott was new and did not have one. "To earn one," she continued, "you need to swim the length of the pool, show me the steps on one side by tapping it with your paw, then swim the length back and show me the steps on the other side. This keeps little runts like you from drowning and saves me the trouble of jumping in after you!"

Then Miss Casey Jane cleared the pool, and Prescott dove in. In and out his head popped just like the ducks had taught him on the farm. He swam fast! His paw hit one step and then he flipped, turned, and pushed, and swam the second lap back as fast as he could!

He stepped out of the pool to hear the howling cheers of Polly and the other dogs. He had proudly earned his swim certificate!

Out of the pool and onto the mats for story time!

Yappy Hour! The time to celebrate dog daycare friends. "So, it's your Whelping Day!" Prescott happily barked back at the barker.

At the end of the day, a voice came over the loud speaker: "Paging, Prescott Red! Paging, Prescott Red! Your Aunt Silver Dapple is here for pick up."

Prescott happily barked a goodbye to his new friends, "See you tomorrow!"

And ran as fast as he could to greet Aunt Silver and tell her about his fun dog daycare day!

Printed in the United States
by Baker & Taylor Publisher Services